**Rodney Finds a Best Friend**

**MILTON & HUGO L.L.C.**
4407 Park Ave., Suite 5
Union City, NJ 07087, USA

Website:      www. miltonandhugo.com
Hotline:      1- 888-778-0033
Email:        info@miltonandhugo.com

Ordering Information:
Quantity sales. Special discounts are available on quantity purchases by corporations, associations, and others. For details, contact the publisher at the address above.

Library of Congress Control Number:    2024912340
ISBN-13:      979-8-89285-154-1      [Paperback Edition]
              979-8-89285-155-8      [Hardback Edition]
              979-8-89285-153-4      [Digital Edition]

Rev. date: 05/30/2024

# RODNEY
## FINDS A BEST FRIEND

### BY
# SHELLEY NEITZEL

One winter day at lunch, Rodney was outside in the school playground. He was sad because he had nobody to play with. He looked around and it seemed as though everyone had a best friend to play with, but not Rodney.

So Rodney went down the slide... alone. He played ball... alone. He ate his lunch... alone. Finally it was time for him to walk home... alone.

Rodney's mom noticed Rodney's face was very sad.

"Rodney, why are you so sad today?" she asked.

Rodney looked up with tears in his eyes... "Mommy,
how do I find a best friend?" he asked.

"Well, maybe you need to look around for one," she said.

"But I don't know what my best friend looks like," Rodney replied
sadly. "And I don't know where to look or how to call one."

Rodney's mom smiled, "Oh Rodney, it's easy to spot one,"
she said. "Tomorrow when you go to the school playground
you need to be observant. That means you must really pay
attention, look around and you will see your best friend."

Rodney was confused. "Will they be tall or short? Will they
wear glasses? Will they have black and white feathers or
brown feathers? Will they be loud and chatty or quiet?"

"You will just know Rodney," said mom
Rodney was still very confused.

The next day Rodney set out towards school Feeling confident that today he would Find his best Friend.

The bell rang at lunch and Rodney ran outside to be observant like his mom had told him. He walked all around the schoolyard, looking for his best friend. He came around the corner and there was a small penguin, sitting on the swing eating his tuna sandwich all alone.

Rodney thought to himself, this looks like it could be my best friend! He waddled confidently towards the small penguin and said, "My name is Rodney...what's your name?"

Very faintly the penguin replied... "It's Lee."

"Hi Lee," he said, "Would you like to be my best friend?"

Lee slowly raised his head and shrugged his shoulders and said, "Sure Rodney...would you like half of my tuna sandwich?"

Rodney was surprised that it was so easy to get a best friend. "Yes please!" he replied.

Rodney and Lee played ball together.

They played hide and seek, they took turns pushing each other on the swings and after school they walked home together.

It turns out that Lee wasn't really very quiet after all. He chatted all the way home, but Rodney didn't mind at all.

Rodney ran into his house
and yelled to his mom...

"This was the best
day ever!!!"

Rodney couldn't wait to see his new best friend at school tomorrow!

The End